grand master little master
series

GW00726912

the Karate tournament

Written by Patricia Merker

Illustrated by Lauren Wilhelm

Foreword

I am pleased to support and boost into form the marvelous content in this Grand Master/ Little Master interactive book series.

I commend talented author Patricia Merker and the sensitive Pick-a-WooWoo publishing team for your combined commitment to bring what I consider universal, peace-making principles into the laps of children and families. This inspired book series combines soul-honoring, character-building, personal-empowerment techniques with balanced mind/body/ spirit activities. The GM/LM series guides children and their families with skillful, playful fun into seeing God as our partner in life. Patricia masterfully brings story into easy living action that articulates in simple and easy-to-live ways how to create a deeply self-inspired AND Divine-inspired lifestyle.

This kind of out-of-the-box educational approach is fundamental to the internationally acclaimed NY Times best selling *Conversations with God (CWG)* series of books and is a mission of the School of the New Spirituality, Inc., the education non-profit founded by author and spiritual leader Neale Donald Walsch.

I'd like to highlight in a concise summary, key principles that the Grand Master/Little Master books bring to life. These foundational beliefs hold inherent power which any parent, grandparent, teacher and all youth professionals may utilize in their work and play with young people to nurture and foster healthy, joyful, loving, honored-for-who-they-are souls:

- God is the All, not any one thing outside of us
- The Divine communicates with us and inside us all the time
- Look for the spark of Source/God, or goodness, in every living being.
- Love is all there is; look inside and see.
- True Love is unconditional, that is it remains without conditions.
- What you CAUSE in the world comes back to you, CAUSE something wonderful today
- Every minute has choice in it. Choose the best for the good of you and for the good of all.
- There is no right or wrong, life is – and we live, learn to love through it all
- Raising children with the belief that they are perfect, magnificent souls on earth will change the world – one healthy child at a time.

As a decade-long co-leader of the School of the New Spirituality, Inc, I professionally endorse Patricia's books. Thank you, Patricia and Pick-a-WooWoo, for this important educational series and contribution to our world.

Linda Lee Ratto EdM, Former Director, Global Education; School of the New Spirituality, Founded by Neale Donald Walsch.

A note from the Author

The Grand Master/Little Master series of books teach, even very young children, about their source of power within. Your child will delight as they follow the journey of the "chosen" little masters in each story. There is no shortage of smiles, admiration and compassion that will warm their hearts and inspire them to re-read these stories over and over.

If however, you choose to take these magical stories to the next level, so begins an interactive adventure in which your child becomes the main character. Minimal parental participation and weekly lessons from Grand Master allow children to address their *own* childhood fears, concerns and self esteem issues.

Universal Laws are presented in ways that give children an opportunity to *experience* their magic rather than to simply read about it. To access the interactive unit of this series which includes how to get started, a synopsis of the lesson associated with each story, a note to the parents, and the weekly lessons from Grand Master to your child, please visit http://www.pickawoowoo.com/childrens-spiritual-books/grand-master-little-master-series/

Enjoy the journey!

Patricia Merker

Patricia can be contacted through her website
http://www.thegrandmasterlittlemasterseries.com/

Saturday morning came way too soon. Haley had a karate tournament at 10:00 am. She was competing in three separate divisions at a local contest. The knot in her stomach got tighter and tighter. Why was she so nervous? *I mean, who cares anyway if I bring home a trophy?* she thought.

Her mother came into the room and, sensing her daughter's nervousness, asked, "Are you okay?"

"No, I'm not!" Haley snapped back. "I'm tired of stupid old karate. It ruins my Saturday mornings. Why can't I just stay home and watch cartoons like other kids?"

Haley could see that 'here we go again' look on her mom's face.

"Do you want to play a game?" asked her mother. *A game,* Haley thought, *at a time like this?* She thought her mother had certainly lost a marble or two, but could not quite resist the temptation.

"Don't know, what kind of game?" she curiously asked.

"Well," her mother said, "I'm not so sure it's a game. You'll have to decide for yourself. Are you ready?"

"Yep," was Haley's unenthusiastic reply.

Her mother's voice became calm and soft. She spoke. "I am one of the Great Grand Masters of the Universe and I am here to tell you that you are a Little Master-in-training."

"Mom?" Haley asked questioningly. "Are you crazy?"

It *sounded* like her mother. It certainly *looked* like her mother. And yet, there was *something* different . . .

"Today," she continued, "I show up as your mother. Tomorrow I could show up as your dad, your little brother, your teacher, or even a bully at school."

"Uh, okay mom. I mean Grand Master, or whoever you are," she giggled. "Is there a point to this game?"

There is a point to everything, Little Master, and you will soon discover that. But for now, we must work on today's lesson. Are you ready?"

"I guess so," replied Haley as she sat upright in bed.

"WHAT YOU GIVE AWAY COMES BACK." Do you understand, Little Master?"

"Not really mom, oh, sorry, I mean, Grand Master," Haley responded with a smirk on her face.

Grand Master continued, "It means that if you want to be happy, make someone else happy. If you want good friends, *be* a good friend. If you want others to share and take turns, *you* must share and take turns. It's very simple. The Universe gives back whatever you *cause* to others. But be *very careful* what you cause, Little Master. Try not to cause sadness or anger or meanness. This too must come back. The Universe is fair, and whether you are aware of it or not, that is how it works."

"I don't get it. What does that have to do with me?" Haley asked.

"It has everything to do with you," said Grand Master, "and today you must **cause** calmness to someone at your tournament. *You* will then be calm. When you are calm, you will be free to do your best."

"And Little Master," she added, "it might be best if this meeting is our secret. Know that I am with you always, even when you think I am not." With that, her mother/Grand Master exited the room.

Haley went through her usual morning routine; slightly preoccupied with this strange new game she was playing. *What does she mean that **I'll** have to decide if it's a game or not?* she thought. *Does she seriously think this is real? Oh well, I can play along!*

"Mom!" Haley yelled, running down the hall from the bathroom,

"What if *I'm* the most nervous kid there? Who will make *me* feel better?"

"What are you talking about honey?" her mother asked, acting as though she'd been in the kitchen the whole time.

Haley rolled her eyes. She ran back to the bathroom and giggled.

They had passed the old hotel many times, but never had Haley seen so much excitement going on! The tournament attracted people of all ages from beginner white belts to seasoned black belts. The noise was nearly deafening from the last minute enrollments and family members trying to find good places to sit. Loved ones were getting their cameras and camcorders ready. It was really quite thrilling!

She felt a part of something big. Maybe she was glad to be here after all. It was hard to tell since she felt like she might lose her breakfast at any minute!

Haley straightened her green belt with shaky hands. She took a seat on the floor, just outside of ring five.

Across the room, sitting on the floor by ring three, was a little boy with a brand new white belt. Haley could tell that this was his first competition. He was hugging his knees to his chest and he looked terribly frightened. *Maybe I should go over to him*, she thought. *Maybe I can help.*

"Hi, my name's Haley, what's your name?" Haley thoughtfully asked.

"David." Replied the little boy, without looking up.

"Where's your mom and dad?" she asked in an attempt to coax him into some conversation. She carefully spied the room for someone who could have brought him. *Why weren't they with him?* she wondered. He was scared, she could tell.

"In heaven," answered David, with a slight quiver in his quite voice.

The knot in Haley's stomach grew to the size of a basketball. ***This*** *is what I get for trying to calm someone else! I thought I was supposed to feel better. Now I have to feel bad for both of us!* she thought. *Grown ups don't know anything.*

"That's probably a better place to be today. It's very crowded here!" said Haley; not believing what just came out of her mouth. "I'd better go." she said, feeling an uncomfortableness that she didn't understand. "Bye, good luck."

She was happy to get back to ring five, where she could continue to worry about her own situation. *I guess my problem is pretty small,* Haley pondered. *I mean, my parents will love me if I win or lose. David's parents won't even know.*

She wondered what it felt like to be without a mom and dad. Having to deal with parents wasn't the easiest thing in the world. Her mother and father were very strict about whom she hung out with, what shows she watched on TV, having homework done on time, and eating healthy foods. Sometimes it seemed that they tried very hard to make her life miserable. And yet, she knew they loved her very much. She was so used to her mom and dad being there. *If suddenly they weren't . . .* she imagined.

Ugh! Back to the tournament! she thought. *I've got to focus. That's what they teach us in karate; focus!*

The harder she tried not to think of David, the more her eyes kept drifting back to the little boy in ring three.

The tournament had started in rings one and two. There were older kids with their sparring equipment on, waiting to be called to the center of the first ring. Haley didn't like sparring much.

She saw her friend Tyler bow before the row of judges in ring two. "Judges, may I begin, please?" she heard him say in a loud, confident voice. *I wonder if he feels that confident,* Haley thought.

Once again, her eyes wandered back to ring three. David was smiling at her. She smiled back, wondering again who brought him and why they weren't here to help him get through this tough event! If she had been alone at her first tournament, she certainly would never have come to a second one!

Almost against her will, she stood up and went back over to him.

"David, listen, I'm a little bit nervous. I always get nervous before these things." Haley said without lying. "Do you have any suggestions? I mean, if *my* parents weren't here, I'd totally fall apart. But you're so brave. You make me feel like I can do it!" Haley said, feeling there was some truth in what she had said. Her stomach suddenly felt better. She really *did* feel like she might get through this tournament after all.

"I just pretend that I'm a super hero!" shouted David, suddenly looking excited to be able to help. "Well actually," he said, "I've never been to a tournament before. But that's what I'm *gonna* pretend!"

For just a moment, Haley had the feeling that if her heart could smile, this is what it would feel like. It was a warm, wonderful sensation to see his face brighten. She felt a sense of pride that she had *caused* something pretty special.

"What a great idea! Do you think *I* could do that too?" asked Haley.

"Sure, I guess so" replied David, smiling gratefully at her.

"Okay David, thanks. It's almost my turn so I'd better go. Can we talk when the tournament is over to see how we did?"

"You bet!" he cried.

Haley *really* didn't like sparring. They had to put on all sorts of padded pieces so they didn't get hurt if they got kicked or punched. They even had to wear a mouthpiece to protect their teeth! It was okay during her karate classes. Her opponents were her friends and no one wanted to be rough. It was like a game. Everyone had fun and laughed a lot. But at a tournament, everything was different. She didn't know the people she was competing against and they didn't smile much. They were *serious* about getting points. It could be pretty scary.

But Haley felt good inside today as she stood up to face her opponents. She felt powerful, as though she had some hidden strength. *Where did it come from? Why had she never felt it before?* She couldn't help but wonder if it had something to do with David.

Her kicks and punches were delivered with more confidence than she could ever remember having. She didn't back out of the ring today, like she usually did. She felt sure of her every move and it showed.

Haley won a beautiful second place trophy in her division of eight-year-old green belts.

It was fun to carry a trophy around after a tournament. People scurry around and find others with trophies to share stories. It makes it all worth while. She didn't always win trophies, of course. It was harder then to feel good.

Where is David? she wondered. She spotted him standing next to a tall, elderly man. "*Maybe that's his grandpa*," she thought.

"Hi David, how'd you do?" asked Haley, seeing that he did not have a trophy in his arms.

"Not as good as you I guess, congratulations," David replied with a forced smile.

Then the most amazing thing happened. Before she could stop herself, Haley stuck the trophy in David's arms and said, "This belongs to you David. I would have totally crashed if you hadn't told me I could do it. So I just wouldn't feel right about keeping it." She couldn't believe what she had just done!

"Really?" asked David. "Really," Haley said, smiling. There was that warm, fuzzy feeling again. It felt like everything was right in the world.

"We are so proud of you honey," said Haley's dad as they walked
toward the door to leave the building. "What you did today for
that little boy is the best kind of special. You make us proud to be
parents! You certainly **caused** a lot of happiness today!"

Caused, . . .there was that word again, she thought. *I did cause
happiness today, didn't I? It's the best kind of feeling.* Although
she thought it might be a little silly, she secretly wondered if Grand
Master would think that she had learned her lesson well.

As she passed through the doorway, the old man with David bent
down to whisper a grateful, "Thanks sweetie."

"My pleasure," Haley whispered back with a smile. And it
certainly was.

Haley felt relaxed now that the tournament was over. The pace would slow down in her karate classes and things would seem normal again. After a competition, she was always glad that she had been a part of it. It made her feel good inside that she had worked so hard. She was thankful to her parents too. After all, they always made sure she went to classes, even though she complained a lot. She was thankful that she *had* parents.

As she lay in bed, she looked up on her shelf at the three other trophies she had won previously. She smiled. All that hard work and hours of practice! But it was so weird; the one that she *didn't* take home today made her feel better than all her other trophies combined. How could that be?

It was kind of funny how it all worked out. She made herself feel better by helping David. Then David felt better because he thought he was making *her* feel better. It was sort of like magic; such a wonderful discovery! Grand Master had been right, or was it her mom? *Was* it a game? It doesn't matter who said it. *It's a good thing to know*, Haley thought, drifting off to sleep.

Haley yawned and stretched. She liked waking up on her own, with no hurry about getting ready for school. She turned over on her stomach, getting ready to drift back off to sleep, when she felt something under her pillow. She pulled it out and read:

Dear Little Master,

You have a very big heart for such a little girl. Today you learned your lesson well. You caused kindness, love, compassion and friendship. These things will all be yours when you need them. And remember, when you need to feel a certain way, cause it for someone else, like you did with David today. Such a wonderful Universal Truth! If more people paid attention to what they caused in the world, they would be so much happier.

Some of the lessons that we work on will be easy to understand. Some will be hard. The important thing to remember is to trust the Universe. There is meaning and purpose to all the lessons, Little Master, I promise. Be patient. Patience is good.

Continue to work hard in school, karate, and everything you do. Continue to love and be good to your family, they are a gift. I will visit you when I need to. Look for me in every living being, that is my home. When you need to feel close to me, close your eyes and feel me in your heart. It will make you smile. Remember that I am always with you, even when you think I am not.

I love you,
Grand Master

Haley ran out to the living room to show her mom and dad the letter. She almost fell on top of her little brother, Jordan, but she thought she would not yell at him today; maybe she would hug him instead. His eyes always lit up when he saw her. "Good morning Jordan!" Haley said as she gave him a big squeeze.

"Good morning Hayey!" he happily responded. You could almost see the 'what's wrong with her' look on his face!

"Look what I got, from my new friend!" Haley said excitedly, very proud of the letter she was holding. Mom and dad read the letter. "This is very nice honey, but I'm a little confused, *who* wrote it?" asked her mother with a silly expression on her face.

"Did you have a friend come over last night when you should have been sleeping?" teased her father.

"You guys!" said Haley. She gave them each a big hug and ran back into her room.

She giggled, and secretly she could hardly wait for the next magical lesson.

Pick-a-Woo Woo

© Copyright 2011

National Library of Australia Cataloguing-in-Publication entry
Author –Merker, Patricia,
Title: The karate tournament / by Patricia Merker; Illustrated by Lauren Wilhelm
Edition: 1st ed.
ISBN 9780980652048 (pbk.)
Series: Merker, Patricia. Grand master, little master; bk. 1
Other Contributors: Wilhelm, Lauren
Dewey Number A8234

Publishing Details
Published in Australia - Pick-A-Woo Woo Publishers
www.pickawoowoo.com

Printed
Lightning Source (US/UK/EUR/AUS)

Channels / Distribution

United States
Ingram Book Company; Amazon.com; Baker & Taylor

Canada
Chapters Indigo; Amazon Canada

United Kingdom
Amazon.com; Bertrams; Book Depository Ltd; Gardners; Mallory International

Australia
DA Information Services; The Nile; Emporium Books Online; James Bennet (Australian Libraries) Dennis Jones and Associates; Brumby Books and Music

Other Books in the Grand Master Little Master Series

Book Two Sink or Swim
Topic: Fear

Grand Master says:
"Everyone has fear at some time in his or her life, Little Master. The choice is whether you have IT or it has YOU.
Choose one, because it *truly* is a choice!"

Sink Or Swim is the second book in *The Grand Master/Little Master series* and addresses the topic of fear. It is highly recommended that you begin this series with *The Karate Tournament*, which is the foundation for all subsequent books in the series, and allows your child to meet Grand Master and be chosen to be a "little master-in-training". It is not necessary to follow in order after book one.

Whatever your child may be afraid of: the dark, heights, monsters in the closet, or flying, etc., they will relate to Haley's crippling fear of the water, and what it costs her to hang on to the fear. This book gives your child an opportunity to observe their fear differently. Both adults and children will find themselves asking the question "Is this fear something that I have, or does this fear have me?

Book Three
Love has many faces.
Topic: Love (in all its forms!)

Grand Master says:
"Love is all there is, Little Master. Sometimes it does not look like love, but it is.
I am *love,* I am *you,*
I am the world and I live inside the soul of every living being.See if you can find me where you think I am not!"

Love Has Many Faces is the third book in *The Grand Master/Little Master series* and addresses the" less than loving" people in our life.

Jordan is anxious to start first grade and can't wait to meet his new teacher! You can imagine his dismay when he realizes that he is to spend an entire school year with a crotchety teacher that is not very nice to the class, and especially seems to not like *him*. Read this heart-warming story of a young boy who follows Grand Master's advice, and looks deeper than the surface to find an expression of love.

CPSIA information can be obtained
at www.ICGtesting.com
Printed in the USA
274586LV00004B

9 780980 652048